Full Steam Ahead

by **Faye Gibbons**

Illustrated by
Sherry Meidell

Boyds Mills Press

Published by Boyds Mills Press, Inc.
A Highlights Company
815 Church Street
Honesdale, Pennsylvania 18431
Printed in China
Visit our Web site at www.boydsmillspress.com

U.S. Cataloging-in-Publication Data
(Library of Congress Standards)

Gibbons, Faye.
Full steam ahead / by Faye Gibbons ; illustrated by Sherry Meidell. —1st ed.
[32] p. : col. ill. ; cm.
Summary: A young boy and his grandpa ride on a steam
locomotive chugging through Georgia one hot summer day.
ISBN 1-56397-858-X
1. Steam locomotives — Georgia — Fiction.
2. Grandfather and child — Fiction.
3. Railroads — Passenger cars — Fiction. 4. Summer — Georgia — Fiction.
I. Meidell, Sherry.   Title.
[E]   21   2002   AC   CIP
2001092183

First edition, 2002
The text of this book is set in 14-point Souvenir.

10 9 8 7 6 5 4 3 2 1

For my grandson,
Matthew Patrick Gibbons,
who always goes full steam ahead!
—F. G.

For my husband, Dave,
twenty-five good years
—S. M.

ME AND MY FAMILY WERE HOEING COTTON. The Georgia mountains were baking under a July sun. So were we.

"Quit playing with that cap and get to work, Sammy," Mama said to me for maybe the twelfth time that day. The train engineer's cap was a birthday gift from Grandpa and the best present I ever got.

"Sammy's dreaming of being a train engineer," teased my older brother, Jimbo, and my big sister, Rose, laughed. I didn't.

The teasing stopped when a buggy came bouncing up to the edge of our field. It was Grandpa. He was waving his hat and grinning big.

"Something wrong?" Papa called.

Grandpa shook his head and his eyes sparkled. "The train's coming through today, 'stead of next week!"

Us young 'uns cheered and dropped our hoes. It was what we'd been waiting for all summer—the first train, a genuine steam locomotive. And it was coming right through Turkey Creek, Georgia!

Rose decided to wear her new bonnet, and Mama said, "I've got to find my good silk handkerchief to wave."

Papa laughed. "Don't take your parasol, Sarah. You'll spook the train."

Grandpa grinned at Jimbo and me. "Want to help me spread the word?"
"Not me," Jimbo answered. "I'm leaving for Tyler Cut right now."
"I'll help," I said and climbed up on the buggy seat beside him.

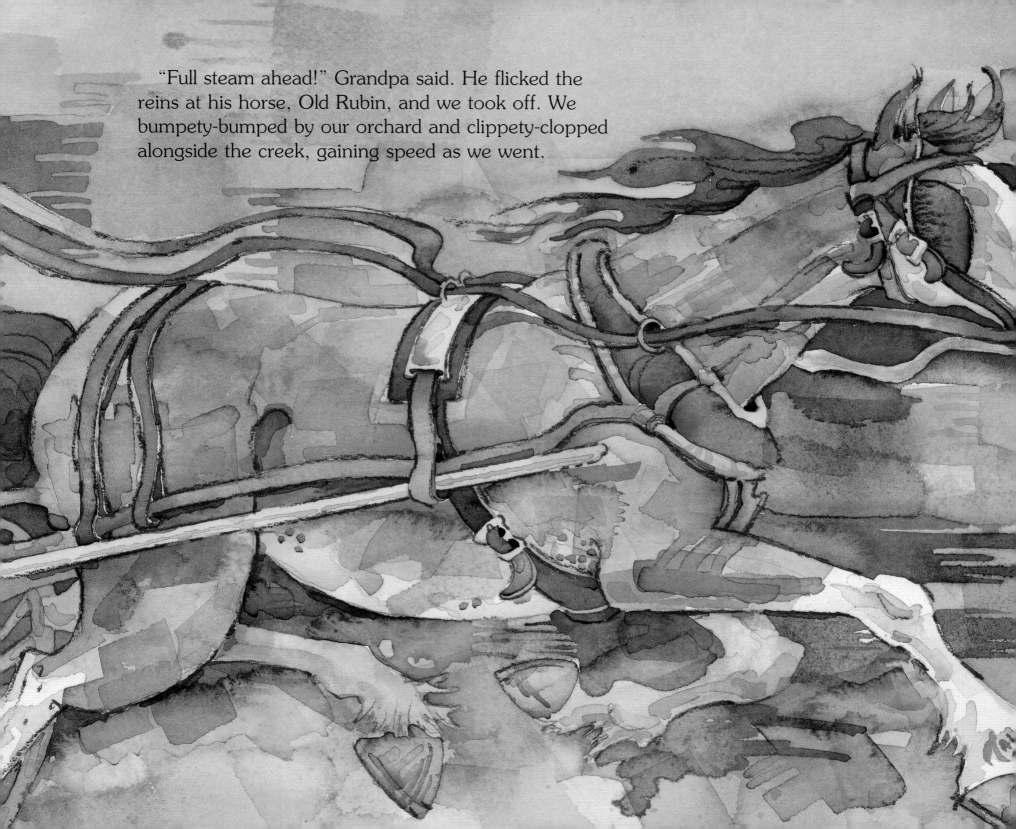

"Full steam ahead!" Grandpa said. He flicked the reins at his horse, Old Rubin, and we took off. We bumpety-bumped by our orchard and clippety-clopped alongside the creek, gaining speed as we went.

"The train's coming through today!" I yelled when we reached the preacher's tidy house and saw the Reverend's wife sweeping her porch.

"Glory be!" Mrs. Nolan cried. She threw down her broom and ran for the front door, shouting, "Ernest, put down that Bible! We have to go!"

We rolled on down the road. "Train's coming through today!"
I hollered when we saw the Blankenship girls gathering green beans
in their garden.

"Yippee!" the girls whooped, and dropped their baskets.

We rolled on, taking a curve on two wheels and clackety-clacking over a truss bridge. "Train's coming through today," I yelled to the Moss young 'uns by the corn mill.

We told the Pucketts, the Deals, and the Hamricks. We told the Willbanks and the Clarks. Then Gramps looked at the sun and swung the buggy around.

But it was too late. We were splashing through a creek when we heard a strange sound in the distance—a low, mournful kind of whistle.

"Whoa!" Grandpa cried, tugging on the reins.

"The train?" I whispered as the buggy stopped, and then I moaned. "We don't have time to get to Tyler Cut."

"The tracks are just a hop and a jump up that way," Grandpa said,
pointing off to the left. "You run on while I tether Rubin."

I scrambled uphill and raced through the woods, looking back every little
bit to see how far behind Grandpa was. Then I heard a *schoof-schoof*,
schoof-schoof, *schoof-schoof*, *schoof-schoof* and forgot all about him.

I came out of the woods, and there was the train, slowing to a stop
at a water tower!
"Land a'mighty!" I said. The sight pure took my breath away.

The locomotive was big as the world. The black metal of it
stretched forever, and it billowed smoke so thick it hid the sky.
The train smelled like tar and oil and steam. It smelled like a
dream come true.

Clunk! Screech!
Taking a deep breath, I ran forward, waving to the engineer leaning out of the engine. I waved to the fireman climbing up on the coal car and reaching for the water chute. I waved to the conductor standing in the doorway of the passenger car.
They waved back.

I heard Grandpa yelling, but I couldn't stop myself. I scrambled down the bank and ran along the railroad bed. "Me and Grandpa couldn't go to Tyler Cut," I told the engineer, " 'cause we had to tell everybody about the train."

The engineer looked at my cap and grinned at the conductor.

"Well, I think we ought to give this young engineer a ride down to the cut," he said.

"Grandpa, too?" I asked, looking back at Gramps, who was puffing his way toward me.

"Why not?" the engineer said. The conductor helped Grandpa down the bank and into the passenger car. I climbed in behind them.

"All aboard!" the conductor sang out.

The train started up with a clank and a lurch that slammed me onto the seat with Grandpa. I got a little scared. What if we passed right by Tyler Cut? What if the train didn't stop?
What if . . .

The wheels began to sing. *Schoooof-schoooof! Schooof-schooof!*
Schoof-schoof, schoof-schoof!

Soon we saw Tyler Cut and all the cheering people waiting there.
The train whistle sounded. *Whoooooooooo! Whoooooooooo!*
"We're stopping!" I said when the train began to clank and lurch.

I leaned out of the window and waved to Mama and Papa, Jimbo and Rose. I waved to the Nolans, the Mosses, the Pucketts, and the Hamricks, and I laughed at the look of amazement on all their faces.

"Tyler Cut!" the conductor sang out. Soon we were out, and Papa
helped us up the bank while everybody cheered.

"How come you got to ride the train?" Jimbo asked.

I pulled myself up tall and looked up the tracks. They were silver ribbons in the sunlight. " 'Cause I'm gonna be an engineer someday," I said. "Just like I dreamed."

"Good for you, Sammy," Grandpa said, clapping me on the back.

I smiled at him and at everybody else. "Full steam ahead!"